Magnus and Friends

Return of the Little Blue Shoe

Written and Illustrated by Christine Renee Hourscht

Magnus and Friends
Return of the Little Blue Shoe

ISBN: 9781098644260

Illustrations, Cover Art & Interior Layout:
Christine Renee Hourscht
www.ChristineRenee.SquareSpace.com

Magnus the Dragonfly Song

Christine Hourscht

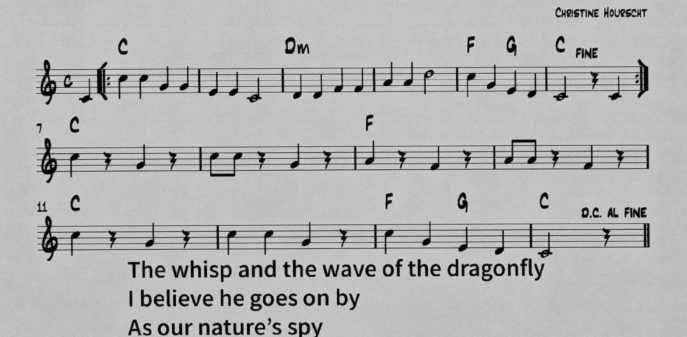

The whisp and the wave of the dragonfly
I believe he goes on by
As our nature's spy

He wanders with curiosity
He likes to fly by the lilies and the trees
And sometimes right by me

Dances, sings, waving his wings
He loves to fly way up high
Orange, green, yellow and blue
Colors he sees 'round you!

His adventures are with his friends
They meet and greet for lots of fun
In the rain or sun

He smiles and laughs while in the sky
Waving hello and goodbye
As he whisps on by

One sunny afternoon…

Magnus the Dragonfly met up with his
best friend Sierra the Bee and

Korbin the Wolf,
Ashley the Rabbit,
and Austin the Owl.

Magnus, Sierra, and Austin were flying around the
top of a tree watching Ashley and Korbin laugh,
jump, and frolic below them.

Suddenly, they all heard a new sound. It was loud, yet whimsical! It was the laughter of a little baby boy. His legs danced in his mother's backpack carrier. His arms swayed like noodles. His head bobbed back and forth. His laughter was contagious. It made them laugh too.

The baby waved at them. "Wow, he can see us!" exclaimed Magnus.

Just then another friend, Snake, slithered out of a hole in the ground. He was half asleep. He yawned and slightly nodded his head toward Magnus and his friends. Then Snake also heard the new sound and looked up and saw the laughing baby boy.

Snake was amazed at the sight of the happy boy wearing the most super cool, blue shoes! Snake's eyes widened and turned many glorious shades of purple and blue. "I *mussssst* have those shoes," he thought to himself. As if by magic, one blue shoe fell on the ground. Snake grabbed it.

Magnus, flying above, noticed that Snake was inching away with the little boy's spectacular blue shoe. "Snake!" cried Magnus. "Stop! You can't take that shoe! That's stealing. It belongs to the boy not you!"

"Oh! I'm *sssso* very *sssssorry*," said Snake as he dropped the shoe.

Magnus, Sierra, and the others knew they had to return the shoe, but how? Where did the baby boy go? As they were gazing at each other puzzling on what to do, they heard a *Knock! Knock! Knock!* from a nearby tree.

"Hi! I'm Woodpecker. Can I help you return the shoe?" the bird asked. Magnus and his friends gratefully agreed.

With Austin the Owl, Woodpecker flew up in the sky to see where the little boy had gone. Yet all they could see were empty trails leading in many different directions.

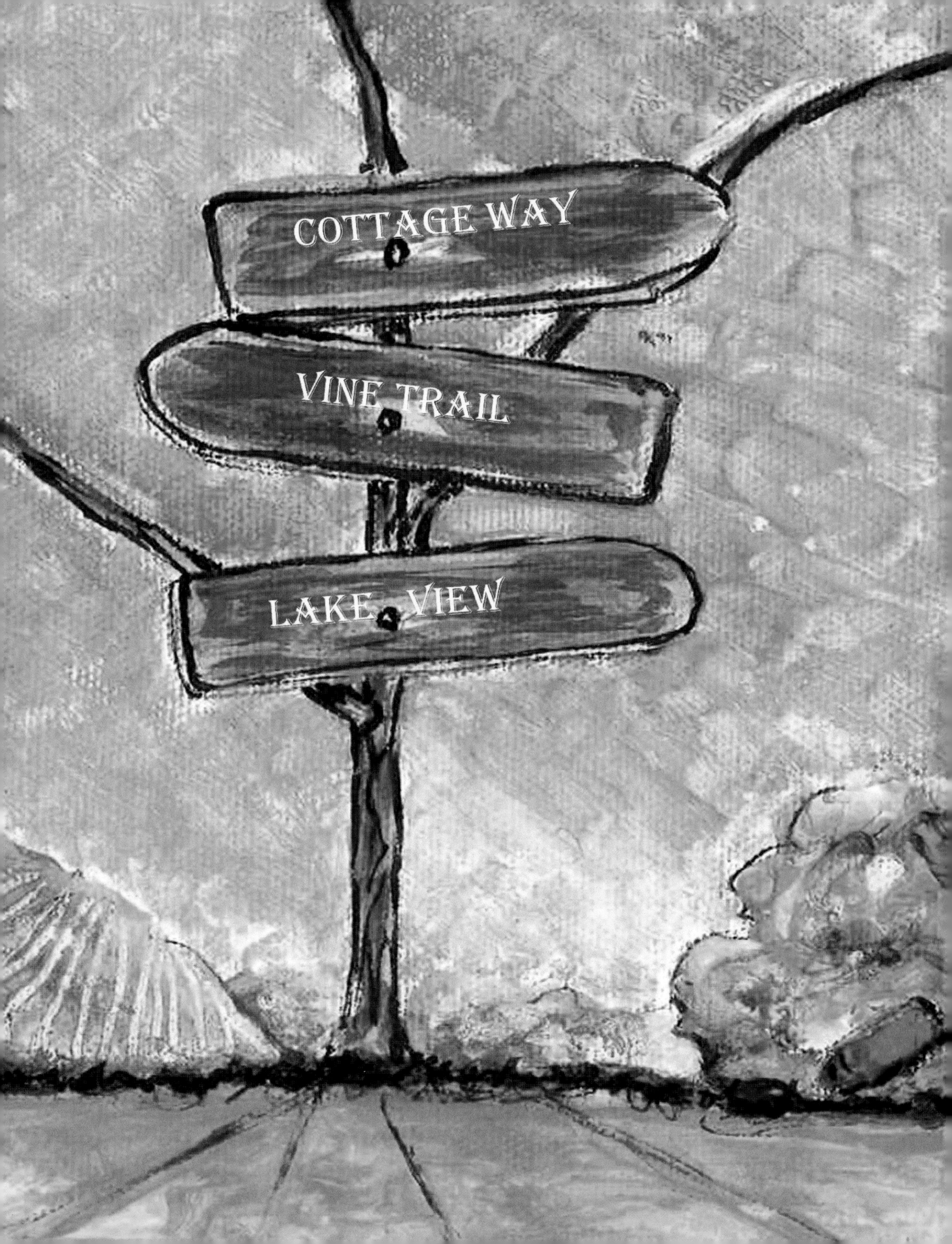
COTTAGE WAY
VINE TRAIL
LAKE VIEW

Korbin the Wolf put his nose to the ground to pick up the boy's scent. He followed a trail until he found a little red bottle laying under a bush. "The baby and his mother went this way!" he called back to the others.

"We need a wagon to carry the shoe and the bottle," said Magnus. "We'll need sticks, vines, leaves, and acorns." All his friends scattered off to find the materials they needed. Magnus always knew what to do.

Everyone returned with something of importance. They worked together to build a wagon with acorn wheels. "What a great team we are," Magnus said proudly.

Korbin the Wolf carefully put on a harness so he could pull the wagon. They jauntily took off down the trail with the shoe and bottle jiggling inside. Korbin stopped abruptly at a bright, glistening lake because the baby's scent had vanished. How could they cross so much water?

Jaeda the Turtle was nearby sunning at the lake. She sang out to them, "Push the purple button on my shell!" They did.

POOF! Suddenly, a bright light circled them as Jaeda's shell opened. This magic light shrank them down so they could all fit inside her shell.

With everyone in her shell, Jaeda slowly walked through the soft, squishy earth at the bottom of the lake. Ashley the Rabbit couldn't stop hop-hop-hopping! Austin the Owl kept hoot-hoot-hooting! Sierra buzzed excitedly. Korbin and Snake smiled. Woodpecker and Magnus fluttered happily. It was like being in an aquarium. They could see through the shell and look at all the fish, frogs, and floating plants swirling around them.

When they reached the other side of the lake, Magnus shouted, "Look!" He pointed to a little cottage. The baby and his mother were sitting on the porch watching ducks on the lake. Magnus and his friends cheered! They excitedly trotted toward the cottage.

The baby saw them. He giggled, kicking his legs and waving his arms. His mother noticed his excitement and looked around. On the ground near the bushes she saw a wagon with the little blue shoe and the red bottle inside. "Oh my! Whoever did this good deed, we are very thankful!" she said. Although she couldn't see the unusual group of friends, the baby could. He smiled and winked at them.

Magnus and friends waved goodbye to the baby.

"Thank you for helping me do the right thing," said Snake to his friends as they returned back toward the lake. "I couldn't have done it without your help."

"That's what friends are for," Magnus assured him. "We help one another in different ways. It's the best way to have great adventures together!"

As a team, they started for home wondering what their new adventure would be.

About the Author

Living in a small town in California, Christine Renee Hourscht is surrounded by nature's beauty. She likes to hike among the trees, admiring flowers, birds, and other animals. She is also enchanted by the ocean, lakes, insects, sky, and fresh air. It fills her with colorful inspiration.

As an artist, Christine is passionate about the beauty of life and lives in gratitude. Her artwork portrays this with whimsical movements, shapes and colors. Her philosophy is to "Live to love" and "Every breath we take is precious." Her artwork is a way to share moments in time.

One morning when a dragonfly whisped and waved near her face, the dragonfly song was born. Magnus's adventures began as Christine visited her favorite magnolia tree and when hiking in wine country.

Special Note from the Author

Dear Readers:

   Thank you for reading **Magnus and Friends Return of the Little Blue Shoe**. This is the next book in Magnus's adventures. I'm looking forward to sharing more with you soon!

Christine

73238609R00020